Mind-Set

by

Joanna Kenrick

Illustrated by Julia Page

First published in 2008 in Great Britain by
Barrington Stoke Ltd
18 Walker St, Edinburgh, EH3 7LP

www.barringtonstoke.co.uk

ISBN: 978-1-84299-523-5

Printed in Great Britain by Bell & Bain Ltd

A Note from the Author

War these days isn't between countries. It's between groups of people who believe different things – and those people can be living next door to each other. Sometimes they even live in the same house.

I wanted to write a story that looked at how people felt about terrorism. It's easy to make up your mind if you're not involved. But what if it happens to you or your family? What if it's your father, your mother, your sister who's been hurt? Then it's not just 'something that happens' – it's *personal*.

And what if the people you care about all believe different things? How do you know which side to be on?

Dedicated to the memory of
Jean Charles de Menezes

Contents

Chapter 1

Bomb

We're in an English lesson when someone's mobile rings.

Mr Hodge is cross. "Whose is that? Mobiles should be switched off in lessons."

Shaleem grins at me. "It's Kelly's," he says softly. "Bet it's her boy-friend again."

"Yeah," I say. "I expect he's dumping her – for the third time this week."

But it's not Kelly's mobile. It's Adam's. He picks it up before Mr Hodge has a chance to get to him. "Yeah?" he says. "What?"

Then an odd thing happens. It's as though he's turned to stone or something. His face just stops moving.

"Turn that mobile off!" shouts Mr Hodge.

But Adam sits there, doing his stone act. Then he drops the mobile. It makes a loud crash as it hits the floor. "I have to go," he says. "There's been a bomb. My dad's in hospital."

And he just gets up and walks out of the room.

****

Right away everyone starts talking. "A bomb? Where? When?"

Some of the girls start crying.

Shaleem looks at me. "Bloody hell, Mark," he says. "What's going on?"

We soon find out. Just before lunch, we're all called into the hall. Mrs Robinson, the Head, looks grim. "Some of you may have heard the news," she says. "There has been a bomb on the Underground. Three bombs, in fact. Lots of people are hurt. If you have parents or relatives who work in the City, you may want to call them to make sure they are safe. If you don't have a mobile phone, you can call from the school office."

Shaleem goes white under his coffee-coloured skin. "I gotta phone my dad," he says. "He's working at the hospital today."

Shaleem's dad is a doctor. He works in a big hospital in the middle of London. My dad drives a lorry – maybe that's why Shaleem is way more clever than me.

It turns out Shaleem's dad is OK, but he can't talk to Shaleem for long because he's dealing with injured people.

There's no point being in school for the rest of the day because all anyone can do is talk about the bombing. We're not even that close to London itself – our school's in Hertford. But lots of people go into the City to work every day. In French, Mrs Collins stops trying to teach us and lets us watch the news on TV instead.

At the end of the day, I say goodbye to Shaleem at the gates. Some of Adam's friends are close by. They look over at us.

"See you tomorrow," I say to Shaleem.

"Yeah."

As I walk away, I hear one of Adam's friends say, "Bloody Muslims."

****

When I get home, Mum is sitting on the sofa, watching the TV. "Did you hear?" she asks.

"Yeah," I say. "Good thing Dad is in France at the moment."

"Is he?" she says. "I didn't know."

"Well, you wouldn't," I say, "as you never talk to him any more."

"Don't go on," she says. "It was all over a long time ago, you know that."

I make myself some toast and sit down with her. The news is all about the bombing – there are gross pictures of burned people and lots of ambulances everywhere.

"An Islamic group has said they carried out the bombing," says the news-reader. "The police are looking into it."

"Islamic?" I say. "Does that mean Muslim?"

"Yes," says Mum. "People who believe in the religion of Islam are called Muslims. Why?"

"Oh nothing," I say. "Just something someone said at the school gates today."

****

The next day, I'm sitting with Shaleem in Maths. I start to notice something odd. The other kids in the class keep looking at Shaleem. "What's going on?" I say.

Shaleem shrugs. "I dunno. Have I got something on my face?"

"Yeah," I say. "Your nose."

Mr Fraser tells us off for laughing.

Adam isn't in school today. But as we walk to Maths, one of his mates pushes past us. Shaleem almost falls over. I grab his arm to help.

"Thanks," he says.

"No problem. What an arse. It looked like he did it on purpose."

Shaleem nods. "Yeah, I know."

I look at him. He bites his lip. "Shaleem," I say, "What's going on? Is there something you're not telling me?"

He pulls a face. "Honest, it's nothing. I just – I think people are starting to look at me funny. Because of the bombing."

"Because of the bombing?" I shake my head. "I don't understand."

"Mark, what planet are you on? It looks like Muslims set off the bombs."

"So?"

"So I'm Muslim."

I blink and shake my head again. "But you didn't have anything to do with it."

"Mark, you are such a dope," says Shaleem. "Of course I didn't. But people can be stupid."

"Not that stupid. No one at school thinks you did the bombing."

"They don't have to. They've already made up their minds. I'm a Muslim, the bombers are Muslim. People will think that I agree with them because we have the same religion."

I pick up my bag. "I think you're wrong. You've always fitted in fine here. Nothing's going to change."

Chapter 2
Taking Sides

We have PSHE that afternoon. Most weeks it's a doss, but today Miss Silva wants to talk about the bombs. "It's important to be able to express our feelings," she says. "It's OK to be worried about bombs."

"I'm not worried about bombs," says Jemma. "I'm worried about Muslims." And she turns to look at Shaleem.

"Well, OK," says Miss Silva, who is a bit taken aback. "Why are you worried about Muslims?"

"Because their religion tells them it's OK to kill non-Muslims," says Jemma. "And they hate us because of the Iraq war."

Shaleem rolls his eyes. "That is such a dumb thing to say," he says. "You don't know the first thing about Islam. And what's the Iraq war got to do with it?"

"It's people like you who are behind all this mess," says Jemma. "You and your kind."

"Uh ..." says Miss Silva. I think she's wishing she hadn't started this now.

"My kind?" says Shaleem. I can tell he's getting mad. "What's my kind? I'm a *person*, just like you."

"You're not like me," says Jemma. "You're not even British."

"He has a British passport," I say at once. "I've seen it."

"Don't be stupid," says Jemma. "That doesn't make him British."

I'm puzzled. "Doesn't it?"

"Oh, leave it, Mark," says Shaleem. "I don't need you to fight my battles for me."

"No," says Jemma. "You've got bombers to do that, haven't you?"

There is a sudden silence. I feel sick.

****

"I know why Jemma said that," I tell Mum when I get home. "She's going out with Adam. His dad was in the bombing. He's still in hospital."

"That's awful," says Mum. "But it doesn't make her right."

The door bell rings. "That's Dennis," she says. "He's coming for dinner."

Dennis is Mum's boy-friend. He's a bit of a drongo, to be honest. I don't understand what Mum sees in him. He's good at football though – nearly got picked for Liverpool when he was my age.

Dennis wants to talk about the bombing too. It was only yesterday and I'm already sick of it. "Bloody Muslim nutters," he says while we eat fish and chips. "Bloody Islam. It turns them all crazy."

"Shaleem says Islam doesn't tell people to kill," I say.

"Who the hell's Shaleem?"

"My friend. You know, from school."

"Oh, *him*," says Dennis, turning to look at me. "You'd better be careful."

"Careful? Why?"

"You can't trust them," says Dennis. "They're all the same."

"Can't trust who?"

"People who run corner shops," says Dennis. "You know – Patels and Singhs. Those people. They come over here and suddenly they're calling themselves British." He mutters something.

"You're not allowed to say that word," I tell him, shocked. "It's racist. Anyway, Shaleem's not from Pakistan. He's from Bangladesh."

Dennis shrugs. "Same thing."

"No it isn't."

Dennis puts his fork down with a crash. "You stay away from kids like him," he says to me. "He's bad news. You'll see. People like him just want to destroy the British way of life."

I look at him. "You're nuts," I say. "You haven't got any idea what you're talking about."

Dennis' face starts to go red. "Don't you dare speak to me like that."

"You don't know anything about Shaleem. He's my mate," I say in a loud voice.

Dennis stands up. He's a big bloke, and he goes to the gym every week. The muscles in his arm are all tight. "Just you listen to me," he says, grabbing my collar. "That Shaleem – he may be your friend now, but you can't count on him. He's not like us. He's different. You'd better remember that."

I struggle but he's too strong. It's getting hard to breathe.

Dennis brings his face close to mine. "You stay away from him," he says, "or he'll drag you down with him."

Then he lets go of me.

Mum sits at the other end of the table, not saying a word.

****

That night, I lie awake for ages. I don't know what's going on any more. Shaleem is my friend. He's always been my friend. What's changed?

I know people can go a bit crazy when bad things happen. I can understand that the kids at school are looking for someone to blame. But it won't last, will it? It'll all blow over soon, won't it?

As I fall asleep at 2am, I remember what Dennis said: "Stay away from him, or he'll drag you down with him."

What does that mean?

Chapter 3

Hatred

The first person I see next day is Adam. He's looking pale and tired, and his eyes are blood-shot. Jemma is hugging him at the school gates. When they see me they both give me the evil eye.

"What's going on?" I ask Rob, another boy in my class.

He looks around to make sure no one's watching. "Adam's dad is still in hospital," he says. "I heard his back is broken. They say he won't ever be able to walk again."

"Honest to God? That's awful. So when will he be coming home?"

But Rob is looking past me and moving away. He doesn't reply to my question. I call after him, but he's talking to someone else.

I shrug and look out for Shaleem. He's late for school, which isn't like him. He's always on time for everything. But today he runs in the door just as the bell goes. Then he sits down and hides his face behind his bag.

"Where have you been?" I say. "And what's the game?"

"No game," he says, his voice muffled.

I tug at the bag. "Shaleem, you OK?"

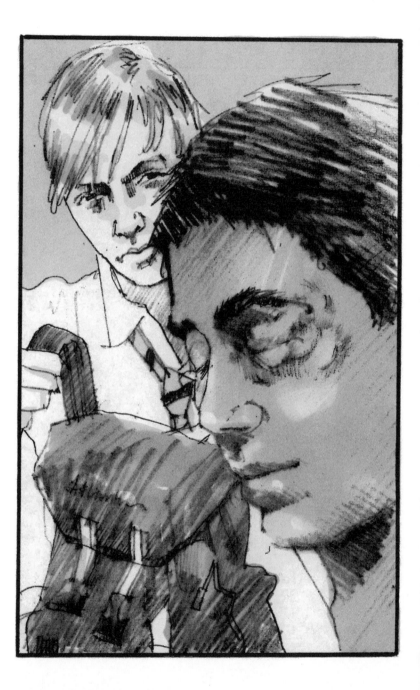

He waits until everyone has gone out of the room before he lets me see. His eye is red, all swollen up and puffy. There's an ugly black mark just under his eyebrow. "Someone punched you!" I say in alarm. "Who did it?"

Shaleem shrugs. "Dunno."

"What do you mean, you don't know? You must know."

He won't look me in the eye. "Didn't see anyone, OK?"

I think he's lying, but there's nothing I can do. We get up to go to our first lesson, but on the way out of the classroom, I trip and fall.

There is a burst of laughter. I look round. Rob is standing in the doorway, his foot sticking out. "Muslim lover," he hisses at me before he heads off down the corridor.

I stand still, feeling the cold creep through me. Shaleem has gone on ahead – he didn't see what happened or hear what Rob said. But I thought Rob was a friend. Why would he say something like that?

I run after Rob, knocking people over along the way. I grab his arm. "What the hell are you talking about?"

He turns to face me. "Oh, come on, Mark. You know how this goes. You can't want to be friends with Shaleem. Not after this."

"What are you talking about? Shaleem had nothing to do with the bombing."

"Yeah, but I bet he thinks it was a good idea. He must do, don't you see? The bombers did it for Islam – that's what they said. Well, he's a Muslim too, isn't he? So that means he's on their side."

"No, it doesn't. Shaleem's not like that. He doesn't think the bombing was right."

Rob takes my hand off his arm and looks me right in the eye. "You'd better decide whose side you're on, Mark. Muslims are our enemies. Shaleem's a Muslim. You can't be friends with us and them. It's one or the

other, Mark. You'd better make up your mind."

Rob isn't the only one to feel like this. As I walk into the class room, everyone – and I mean *everyone* – turns to look at me. And then I hear it – a low hissing, like a hundred snakes. I can't tell who's making the sound, but it could be any number of people. Apart from Shaleem, of course, who sits looking at me, silently asking me for help. As I take a step towards him, the hissing gets louder. I stop. The hissing gets softer.

I take a seat near the window, away from Shaleem. The hissing stops suddenly. I lower my head so that I don't have to see Shaleem's face.

In the next lesson, I sit well away from Shaleem again. I don't know what to do. He's my friend – he's always been my friend – but if I stay friends with him, then everyone else at school will hate me. I don't want to lose my other friends. I don't want to be the one they pick on. But I also feel ashamed that I can't stand up to them. I'm not a strong person.

Chapter 4

Time to Choose

By morning break, Shaleem has shrunk into himself. He looks smaller somehow. As we go out into the play-ground, I can hear the other kids saying spiteful things to him. His shoulders hunch up, and he looks at the ground.

Then, when the others go to play football, Shaleem comes over to talk to me. I look around, but no one is watching.

"Mark," says Shaleem. "Why are you doing this?"

I feel really bad. "You don't understand," I say, scuffing my shoe on the tarmac. "I'm not doing it to be mean to you."

"I understand all right," says Shaleem. "You're just a wimp. You know this is wrong. You know they're wrong. But you're too yellow to stand up to them. You won't fight the stupid mind-set."

I don't know what to say because I know he's right.

"Hey! You!"

We turn. Adam and his mates are standing there. Adam has this frozen look on his face, like he really hates Shaleem.

He uses the same word Dennis did. My fists clench.

"I'm from Bangladesh," says Shaleem in a tired voice. "I told you."

Adam reaches out and grabs Shaleem's shirt. "I don't care where you're from, Muslim. I'm going to make you wish you were back there."

I hear a small voice say, "Leave him alone, he hasn't done anything to you," and it's me talking.

Adam swings around to look at me. "Oh yeah? It's because of people like him and his bloody religion that my dad will be in a wheel-chair for the rest of his life."

"This has nothing to do with Islam," Shaleem mutters.

Adam is still looking at me, anger making his eyes hard. "You'll stay out of this, Mark, if you know what's good for you. This isn't about you. But if you get in my way, you'll get hurt."

"Mark ..." As Adam grips him, Shaleem twists to look at me.

"It's too late for all that now," says Adam, and smashes his fist into Shaleem's face.

Shaleem goes down – and within five seconds bodies are piling on top of him, punching, kicking, scratching. It's a nasty fight. I take a few steps back to get out of the way. I do it without thinking. They're not after me. I should keep out of this.

And then, for a moment, I catch sight of Shaleem's face. It is covered in blood, and it looks like his nose is broken. He curls into a ball on the ground as feet slam into his ribs,

his back, his head. The mob of kids is yelling and screaming.

There is something tight inside me. Shaleem is my friend. He doesn't deserve this. He's a good person. Everyone knows that really. I should wade in – try to help him.

But if I do, they'll do the same to me. There are so many of them. I'm scared.

I stand, unable to make up my mind, watching my friend get beaten up. The longer I wait, the worse it gets.

What am I going to do?

Barrington Stoke would like to thank all its readers for commenting on the manuscript before publication and in particular:

Richie Ahern

Ryan Ahern

Liam Benney

Laetitia Billington

Amy Cooper

Emma Griffiths

Conner Hall

Chloe Hardy

Judy McGurn

Joe McKnight

Margaret Sharratt

William Anderson Smith

Become a Consultant!

Would you like to give us feedback on our titles before they are published? Contact us at the email address below – we'd love to hear from you!

info@barringtonstoke.co.uk
www.barringtonstoke.co.uk

Great reads – no problem!

Barrington Stoke books are:

Great stories – from thrillers to comedy to horror, and all by the best writers around!

No hassle – fast reads with no boring bits, and a story that doesn't let go of you till the last page.

Short – the perfect size for a fast, fun read.

We use our own font and paper to make it easier to read our books. And we ask teenagers like you, who want a no-hassle read, to check every book before it's published.

That way, we know for sure that every Barrington Stoke book is a great read for everyone.

Check out www.barringtonstoke.co.uk for more info about Barrington Stoke and our books!